Tom and Pippo and the Washing Machine

PIPPO

HELEN OXENBURY

ALADDIN BOOKS
Macmillan Publishing Company • New York

One day Pippo played in
the mud and got
really dirty.

Mommy said we
would have to put him in
the machine with the wash.

I said goodbye to Pippo because
I thought he might never come
out of the machine.

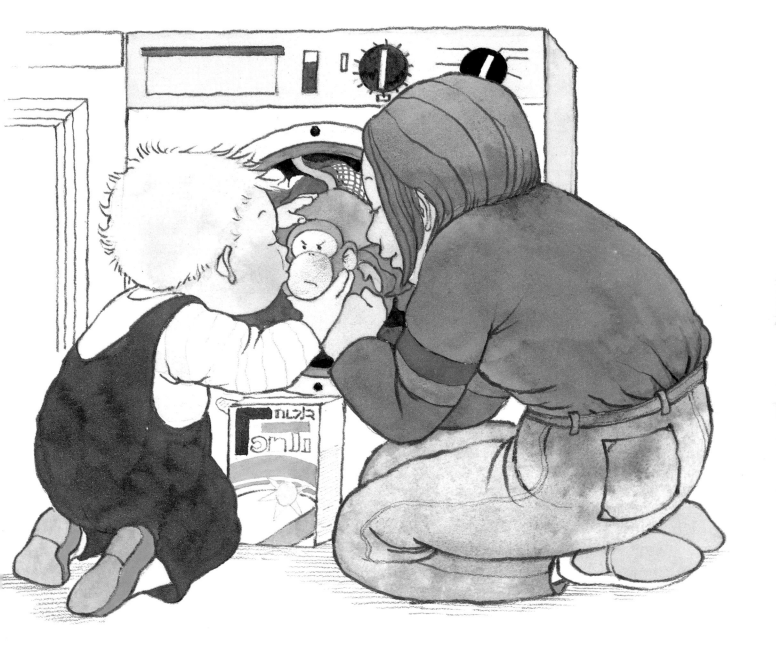

Poor Pippo went
around and around.
I hoped he didn't
feel sick.

When Pippo came out of the
machine, he was really wet.
"Will Pippo ever get dry?"
I asked Mommy.
Mommy said he'd be dry
soon if we hung
him on the
clothesline.

I told Pippo he'd be dry
by bedtime if the
sun came out
and the
wind kept
blowing.

The trouble is, I know Pippo's
going to get dirty again.
I can't keep him from playing
in muddy places.